THE EMPIRE STRIKES BACK

EGMONT
We bring stories to life

This edition first published in Great Britain 2017
by Egmont UK Limited, The Yellow Building,
1 Nicholas Road, London W11 4AN.

© & TM 2017 Lucasfilm Ltd.

ISBN 978 0 6035 7419 1
68483/1
Printed in Estonia

To find more great *Star Wars* books, visit www.egmont.co.uk/starwars

Stay safe online. Any website addresses listed in this book are correct at the
time of going to print. However, Egmont is not responsible for content hosted by
third parties. Please be aware that online content can be subject to change and
websites can contain content that is unsuitable for children. We advise that all
children are supervised when using the internet.

THE EMPIRE STRIKES BACK

Adapted by Geof Smith
Illustrated by Chris Kennett

please   give   back!

A long time ago in a galaxy far, far away . . . .

It is a dangerous time for the Rebel Alliance. After destroying the Death Star, they are on the run from the evil Imperial forces. Princess Leia has led the rebels to a secret base on Hoth, a snowy ice planet. Luke Skywalker rides his tauntaun across the frozen wasteland, on the lookout for bad guys.

An angry snow creature called a wampa attacks!
Luke fights the beast with his lightsaber.

ROAR!

As he escapes, Luke has a vision of Obi-Wan Kenobi.
Obi-Wan tells him to go to the planet Dagobah and
find a great Jedi Master named Yoda.

Not far from the base, Han Solo and Chewbacca spot an Imperial probe droid hunting for the rebels.

BOOM!

Han shoots the droid with his blaster. The droid is destroyed, but Han knows it has signalled the Empire with the location of their hideout.

The Imperial forces have found the rebel base!
Thump-thump-thump! Giant AT-AT walkers march
across the snow.

Zoom! Rebel snowspeeders fight the hulking machines. Lasers have
no effect, but Luke trips an AT-AT with his speeder's tow cable.

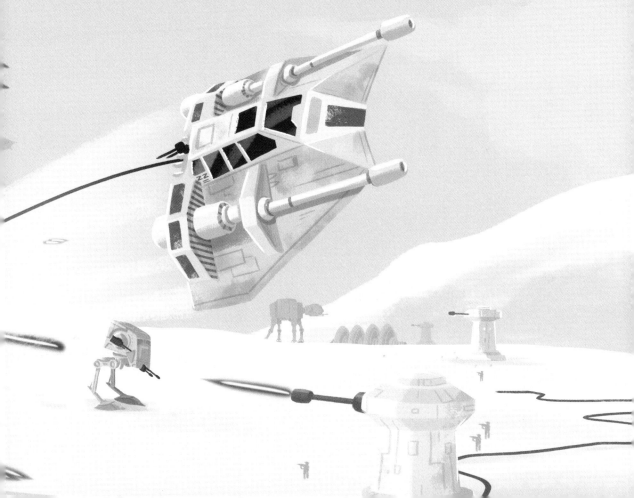

Han Solo, Princess Leia, Chewbacca and C-3PO race to the *Millennium Falcon* – but the ship won't start! "Would it help if I got out and pushed?" Leia asks.

Luckily, the *Falcon* zooms away just as Darth Vader
and his stormtroopers overrun the base.

Luke and R2-D2 escape, too. On Dagobah, Luke finds Yoda and asks the powerful Jedi Master to train him in the ways of the Force.

Luke's training is difficult. He runs and jumps and swings on vines – all with Yoda on his back!

Suddenly, Luke's X-wing fighter begins sinking into
the swamp! He tries to raise it with the power of the
Force but can't. "It's too big."
Yoda is disappointed.

The little green Jedi Master closes his eyes, points his claw . . .
and raises Luke's X-wing using the Force!
"Size matters not," Yoda says.

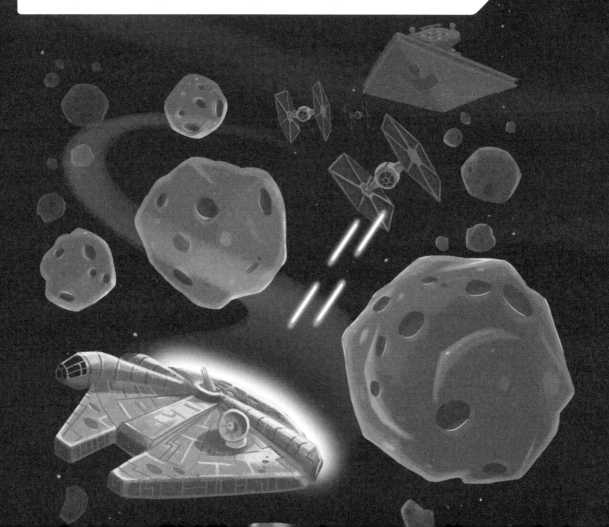

Meanwhile, the *Millennium Falcon* is being chased by Imperial Star Destroyers. Han Solo has a plan to escape. He flies into an asteroid field!

"They'd be crazy to follow us," Han says.

The giant Imperial Star Destroyers can't follow the *Millennium Falcon*, but smaller TIE fighters can.

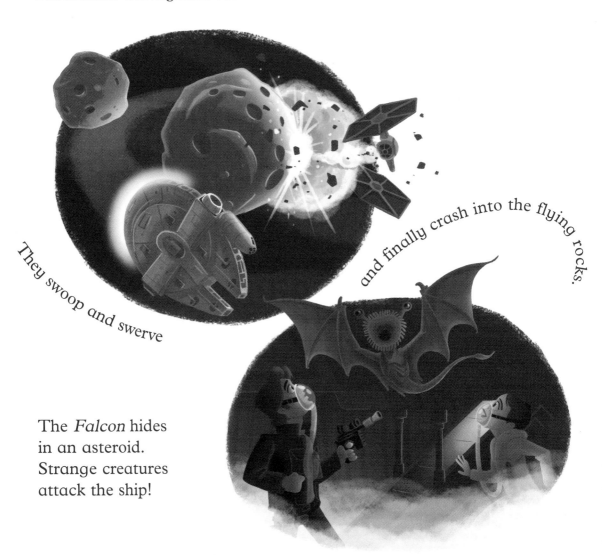

They swoop and swerve

and finally crash into the flying rocks.

The *Falcon* hides
in an asteroid.
Strange creatures
attack the ship!

The *Millennium Falcon* escapes
before it is eaten by a
GIANT SPACE SLUG!

Determined to catch the rebels, Darth Vader hires bounty hunters to find them. The bounty hunters are a cruel and dangerous bunch. The most dreaded hunter is the ruthless Boba Fett.

Han Solo flies the *Millennium Falcon* to the cloud city of Bespin. He hopes his old friend Lando Calrissian can help them. Han doesn't know that they are being followed . . . by Boba Fett!

Lando gives Han and his friends a warm welcome.
But something isn't right . . . Darth Vader and Boba
Fett are waiting for them!

Across the galaxy on Dagobah, Luke feels a disturbance in
the Force. He knows Han Solo and Princess Leia are in trouble.
Yoda tells Luke that he's not ready to face Darth Vader alone.
But Luke knows he must help his friends.

Back on Bespin, Han Solo is frozen in carbonite.
Fwoosh!
Boba Fett claims his prize as Darth Vader sets a
trap for Luke Skywalker.

Luke arrives on Bespin and faces Darth Vader.
Zhip! Zlash! Their lightsabers sizzle as the battle
begins! The Dark Lord wants Luke to join the Empire
and the dark side of the Force.
"Never!" Luke cries.

Before defeating the young Jedi, Darth Vader reveals
a terrible secret. "Luke, I am your father!" he announces.
"Join me, and together, we can rule the galaxy!"
"Noooooo!" shouts Luke. He leaps into a deep tunnel and falls down,
down, down . . . and out of Bespin.

Luke clings to a weathervane
underneath Bespin.
He uses the Force to call to
Princess Leia for help.

Meanwhile, Lando helps Leia, Chewbacca and the droids make a
daring escape on the *Millennium Falcon*.
They quickly save Luke and flee the cloud city.

Luke and his friends rejoin the rebels. They are safe for now, but they know they must save Han Solo from Boba Fett and defeat the evil Darth Vader . . .

THE END